A CIRCLE OF FRIENDS

By Giora Carmi

Star Bright Books
New York

Designed by Jin Choi

Library of Congress Cataloging-in-Publication Data

Carmi, Giora.
    A circle of friends / by Giora Carmi.
        p. cm.
    Summary: When a boy anonymously shares his snack with a homeless man, he begins a
cycle of good will.
    ISBN 1-932065-00-8
    [1. Sharing--Fiction. 2. Stories without words.] I. Title.

PZ7.K1425Ci 2003
[E]--dc21
                                                            2002042879